THE ADVENTURES OF PIRATESS TILLY

Written by Elizabeth Lorayne   Illustrated by Karen Watson

For Alex, Connor + Lochland,
Keep exploring!
Elizabeth Lorayne

white wave press

For my hearts,
R.L. and V.L.
~ E.L.

To all who follow their dreams
~ K.W.

She sails the high seas
With her band of skilled brothers
Piratess Tilly

A great worldly crew
Each found wandering the docks
Sailing ship Foster

From seven countries
The brothers form a tight bond
All loving Tilly

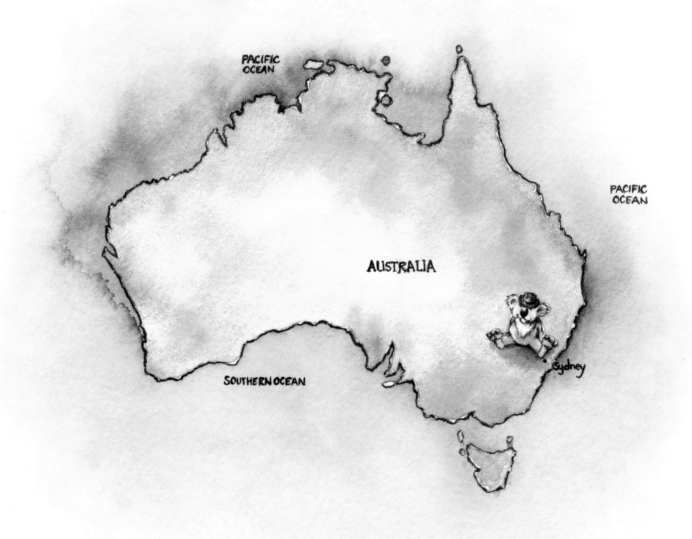

PACIFIC
OCEAN

PACIFIC
OCEAN

AUSTRALIA

SOUTHERN OCEAN

Sydney

She rescued her friend
A happy marsupial
Koala Yuki

Patches head to toe
A network of history
Her clothing scrapbook

Strung on red ribbon

Best tool for adventuring

An heirloom compass

Yuki navigates
From the moonlit stars above
A nautical chart

Together they roam
Day and night observing life
Young naturalists

Staterooms full of books

Darwin and Potter inspire

Lofty dreams unfold

Hoisting the mainsail
The Galápagos Islands!
Tilly at the helm

Wind in Tilly's hair
Nowhere better to study
Nature as teacher

Many days passing
Best used for examining
What would Darwin think?

Yuki mixes paints

Tilly sketches artifacts

Cataloging finds

On red plush pillows
They study their specimens
All safe in glass jars

These long days at sea
Require them to snuggle
Warm in their cabins

Morning approaches
Broken shells scattered topside
Success, "Land ahead!"

Such a striking scene
Black lava rock and lagoons
Views beyond compare

Just off the port side
Magnificence of the sea
Humpback whales surface

Look up and follow
Black wings and beaks full of fish
Blue-footed Boobies

Distant playful cries
Watch the sea lions play catch
Marine iguanas

On oceans so blue

They find exploits aplenty

Studying sea life

"What's that? Over there!"

Eight pairs of eyes following

Yuki's outstretched arm

Pirates smuggling
Baby Giant Tortoises
Adventure awaits

"We must rescue them!"
Team Foster draws up their plan
Moonlight at their backs

Rainfall masks their cause
Rowing their dragon boat launch
Dangerous pursuit

Best plan of attack
Scurry up the anchor line!
Into cannon bays

Stealthily searching
They find the trembling babies
Messy pirate ship

Surfing on their heels
Down lines and into the launch
Rescue accomplished!

Can't delay too long

More expeditions ahead

Happy reunion

Good night, dear Yuki

Sleep well, strong crewmate brothers

Until tomorrow . . .

Printed in China

First Printing, 2014

ISBN 978-0-692-29610-3

White Wave Press
Newburyport, MA

WhiteWavePressBooks.com
PiratessTilly.com